Searching
for Jamila

Written by Sufiya Ahmed
Illustrated by Lia Visirin

Collins

Chapter 1

It was the summer of 1927 and the surging
sea breeze tugged at the blond hair of the identical
boys as they gripped the ship's railing.
Despite the tumultuous waves beneath them,
the 13-year-old twins, Alex and Matt, could barely
contain their excitement.

"Look, Lizzie!" Alex glanced over his shoulder
at his eight-year-old sister standing behind him.
"There's England!"

"Look, Jamila!" Lizzie said in turn, pulling on
the soft hand of her ayah. "That's our home."

Jamila tightened the shawl around her shoulders
and attempted a small smile. The journey from
India to England had taken nearly a month,
and although she'd kept them busy with books
and games, they were now ready to step off
their steamship.

Lizzie pulled free of Jamila to stumble towards
her brothers. Matt grabbed her hand and guided
it to the railing so she could steady herself.
The children swayed to the ship's rocking motion
as Jamila staggered forward. Another gust of wind
and the tidy bun at the nape of her neck almost
came undone. Jamila grimaced and readjusted
the pins in her hair.

"The journey was so much fun," Matt said. "The best part was our stopover in Egypt."

Jamila smiled at him. Matt was her favourite of the Curtis children. He had a gentler nature, more considerate than Alex and Lizzie.

"I loved the pyramids at Giza," Matt continued. "I'm going to become an archaeologist when I grow up."

"I liked the camel ride," Lizzie piped up. "It was so bouncy! But I'm glad I wasn't sitting on Alex's camel."

All four laughed at the memory of Alex's ride. The camel owner had asked if Alex wanted a boring or exciting experience.

In true Alex fashion, he'd shouted "exciting" and on cue, the owner had raced forward with the camel's lead in hand. Jamila had stared, horrified, as Alex bobbed towards the horizon, holding on tightly.

"That was brilliant!" he'd declared, exhilarated, when the camel finally came to a halt.

"*That* was extremely dangerous," Jamila had scolded, shivers running down her spine despite the hot desert heat. Memsahib Curtis had warned Jamila about Alex's reckless streak.

Jamila was employed by Sahib Curtis to accompany the children back home after their Indian summer holiday at their parents' house. Sahib Curtis served as an officer of the British Empire and he and Memsahib lived in the city of Bombay.

A big wave rose and slammed against the ship's side, splashing them with icy jets. Jamila gasped as the water hit her face. She grabbed Lizzie's hand to stop the little girl being swept overboard. "Come on," she urged.

All four staggered away from the railing to the bench that was nailed to the deck.

"I'm going to miss India so much," Alex grumbled. "I'm going back as soon as I can."

"I'm coming too," Lizzie announced. "We'll all go together."

"I may not want to return to India for a while," Jamila teased. "I want to explore new places."

"You can do that," Matt said. "But you must always return to us because you belong with our family."

Jamila laughed, basking in the affection from her three charges. Aged 19, she was only six years older than the twins, and although they respected her as their ayah, they were also friends.

"Well, you won't need me forever, but I'll always be here for you if you do. Now, let's get our belongings packed in the cabin so we're ready to leave this ship. England, here we come."

Chapter 2

The sun shone through the large windows into
the dining room of 222 Old Clover Road. The three
children around the tea table ate silently under
the sharp gaze of the elderly lady in the head seat.
The meal would have ended without a single word being
uttered if Lizzie had not reached for a bun.

"Don't stretch out like some common girl," Granny rebuked, her grim expression turning even grimmer.

"Sorry," Lizzie mumbled, looking down at her plate.

Granny drew a long breath as if to calm her irritated nerves. "I'm not convinced this trip to India was good for you. All of you seem to have mislaid your manners. Did your mother let you run wild there?"

Alex looked up from buttering his scone. "We had a brilliant time, actually. Mother let us have lots of fun. We saw elephants, played cricket on Bombay beach and swam in the sea. It was the best."

"Why am I not surprised at my daughter's lack of discipline!" snorted Granny. "I suppose she didn't sit you down for any lessons either."

"We were on holiday," Alex retorted. "Who does sums in the summer?"

Granny's mouth tightened as she poured tea from the pot.

Matt glanced at the door. "Where's Jamila? She always eats with us."

"Who is Jamila?" Granny asked.

"The Indian girl who was with us yesterday," Matt explained, with a concerned frown. "She's the daughter of the housekeeper at the house in Bombay. Mother asked her to look after us on our trip."

"Ah, the nanny," Granny sniffed. "I noticed that she doesn't have the education to even address you correctly."

Alex stared, confused. "How should she have addressed us?"

"You boys as Master Alexander and Master Matthew, and your sister as Miss Lizzie."

"Mother didn't want her to be formal with us," Matt said. "She said Jamila should be our friend."

"The girl was an employee and should have addressed you correctly," Granny snapped. "Don't my servants in this house address you with the appropriate amount of respect?"

Lizzie noticed that Matt had suddenly gone very still. "What is it?" she whispered.

A look of alarm crossed Matt's face as he jumped to his feet. "What have you done with Jamila?"

"Sit back down!" Granny ordered. "I won't have this insolence."

Matt bristled but obeyed. The tension in the room crackled but he repeated the question. "Where is Jamila?"

Granny glared at Matt. "She has been dismissed."

Alex's butter knife clanked onto the plate. "What?"

"I beg your pardon, not 'what'," Granny corrected sharply. "Anyway, you're too old to need a nanny! Are you babies?"

The children stared at her. Finally, Matt found his voice. "What did you say to her?"

Granny fingered the pearl brooch pinned at the neck of her high-collared blouse. "I merely dismissed her. I do it all the time with servants whose services I no longer need."

"But she wasn't a normal servant from London," Matt cried, his voice rising with each word. "She is thousands of miles away from her home. You've made her penniless and homeless!"

"Matthew Frederick Curtis!" Granny exploded. "I won't have another word out of you."

Matt crossed his arms, but he knew better than to say anything more. Granny was quite capable of grounding him for the rest of the holidays.

"Granny," Lizzie said in a timid voice, "Jamila doesn't know anybody here. She has nowhere to go."

"I'm sure your father paid her," Granny snapped. "She can make her way back to India."

Alex darted a look at Matt's set lips and realised that he'd better speak up. "Father said to make sure you pay her on our arrival."

"Nobody told me!" Granny said, exasperated now. "And anyway, why is your father asking me to pay for his staff?"

"The money was in the letter we handed to you last night," Alex said.

"Well, I haven't opened it yet," Granny said, waving her arm in dismissal. "And why should the girl be paid for her chance at adventure? She should be grateful for being allowed to sail on a steamship. She saw half the world on that journey. Even I haven't had that privilege."

"Mother says that's because you don't like foreign places," Lizzie muttered.

"That's enough!" Granny exploded again. "All three of you to your rooms now!"

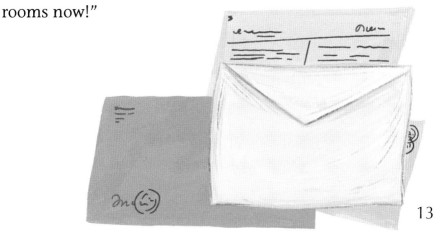

13

Chapter 3

Jamila pulled her shawl tightly around her shoulders as she walked on the cobbled stones. It was dark now and chilly. She'd been walking all day and the streets of London were not how she'd imagined them at all. The big, nice houses on Old Clover Road soon gave way to greyer, cramped ones on overcrowded streets. To Jamila's relief, nobody paid her the slightest bit of attention as she passed them in her sari and sandals, clutching her duffel bag.

Every now and then, Jamila checked the secret pocket in her underskirt. Her passport was hidden there. On this day, it was her most valuable possession. She knew she wouldn't be able to travel home without it.

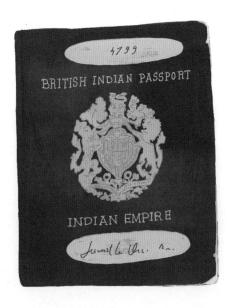

15

An hour or so later, glancing around, Jamila's brown eyes filled with fear as she noticed that there were fewer women and children out now. She swallowed hard, determined not to break down in tears. She needed to focus on reaching her destination after being thrown out of the Curtis household.

Suddenly, someone in a hurry banged into her and she let out a frightened scream.

Turning on her heel, she raced away as fast as she could, unsure which way she was heading. When she could run no more, she dropped her duffel bag and bent over, clutching her knees for support.

Slowly, her breathing steadied and the stitch in her side subsided. Straightening up, Jamila looked around. She was standing in a dead-end street. The end was blocked by a high wall by which an old woman sat huddled on the ground by a makeshift fire.

The old woman had a scarf tied around her head and was wrapped in two shawls.

Jamila hurried towards her. Perhaps she would take pity on a, lost homeless girl.

"Hello," Jamila said tentatively. "May I share your fire?"

"The more the merrier, girlie," the old woman said with a grin, revealing a missing front tooth.

Jamila dropped down onto the pavement and felt the cold through the thin fabric of her sari. She shifted closer to the crate burning with wood, hoping the orange-red flames would warm her. It hadn't been so chilly in the daytime, but the warmth had disappeared along with the sun.

17

Reaching into her duffel bag, she pulled out two little packets of peanuts. She always carried snacks for the children.

Well, she wasn't ever going to see the children again so she might as well eat the peanuts. Jamila held out a packet to the old woman. "For you."

"Thank you, dearie."

They both munched their peanuts.

"You alone?" the old woman asked.

Jamila nodded.

"The streets are no place for young things like you."

Jamila didn't say anything. The darkness soon crept up and the only light in the street came from the flames. Closing her eyes, Jamila swallowed the lump that had formed in her throat. The old woman's kindness had reminded her of Ammi, her mother.

Ammi had begged her not to take the job when Memsahib had offered it, but Jamila hadn't listened.

"Ammi," she'd declared. "It'll be an adventure. How many girls from Bombay get the opportunity to travel to England? That magical land of green hills and fields."

"Only the Sahib describes his country like that," Ammi reminded, worry in her eyes. "Anyone from India who has visited England speaks of a cold place full of factories, workhouses and hardship."

"I refuse to believe it," Jamila insisted. "Think of the money, Ammi. It will come in handy now that Papa is gone."

Ammi had granted permission in the end. There was no doubt that the money would come in handy with raising her two younger daughters now that she was a widow.

Jamila's heart was heavy at the thought of returning to India without her wages. She should have demanded the money upfront from Sahib Curtis. Her failure to do so had now left her penniless.

Chapter 4

Warming her hands by the small flames, Jamila thought
back to her first night in London.

The children had been sent to bed early and Jamila,
just as exhausted, had crawled into the narrow bed
in the tiny room she'd been given. The top floor of
the house was cold, but the blanket had been thick
and warm. Jamila snuggled deep inside and fell into
heavy, exhausted sleep.

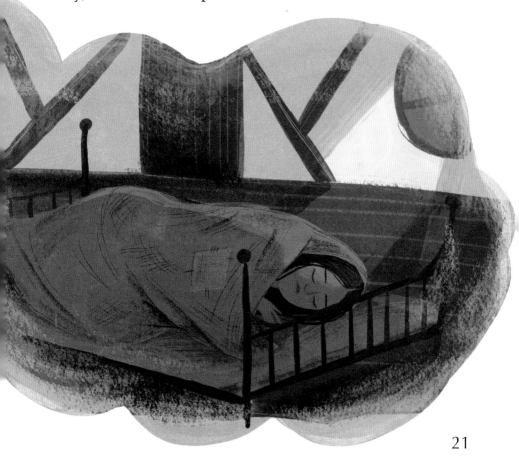

The next thing she knew, she was being shaken by a maid at five in the morning and ordered downstairs. Unsure what was expected of her before the children awoke, she'd sat at the kitchen table and gratefully received the hot drink the cook had offered.

Jamila had swallowed the first sip and managed to keep the disdain off her face. The brew tasted awful.

In India, tea was brewed to boiling point and then allowed to simmer for at least half an hour. In the Curtis house, everyone, including the servants, drank only Kashmiri pink tea which was made of tea leaves, cinnamon, baking soda, salt and almonds. It was the speciality of the cook, Shaqil. Memsahib had met the green-eyed man on her vacation in Kashmir.

The Indian summer fell in the month of May, rather than August as it did in England. As Bombay became unbearable with the heat, all the English retreated to the Himalayan foothills for relief from the scorching sun. The most popular destination town was Simla or "Little England" as it was called. It was where all the important Sahibs and Memsahibs gathered for picnics, garden fêtes, polo games and cricket.

Last year, however, Memsahib had insisted on choosing a different location. An army officer at one of her parties had bragged that Kashmir, high up in the mountains, was the most beautiful place in the world. Tempted by the thought of a place more stunning than the Swiss Alps, the plan had been made to summer in Kashmir.

Jamila was part of the Memsahib's entourage and had gasped in wonder at the sight before her. Kashmir was indeed the most beautiful place in the world.

Jamila grimaced as she took another gulp. She would have to adapt now to this English drink. That's what people with adventurous spirits do. Jamila was hoping she'd be able to visit Scotland too. She'd met many Scottish memsahibs who visited the Curtis house and often talked about the beauty of the highlands. She'd wait till next summer when the weather warmed as it was meant to be very, very cold up there.

"Ahem."

Jamila's thoughts were interrupted by the butler peering down at her from his great height.

"Have you finished?"

She nodded and then stared perplexed at her duffel bag by his feet. Why had he removed it from her room?

"The Mistress no longer requires your service," he informed her in a cool voice. "You may leave now."

Jamila's heart skipped a beat. "Leave?"

"Yes."

Her mouth was suddenly so dry that it felt like she was back in the hot desert by the pyramids in Egypt. She stood up on shaking legs and managed in a suffocated voice: "I want to see the Mistress."

He gave her an incredulous look. "That's not possible."

"I'm not going anywhere until I've spoken to her," Jamila burst out, near to tears.

The butler scowled before marching off.

Jamila slumped down and tried to control the shaking of her limbs. What did the Mistress mean by saying she had to leave? Where would she go? Memsahib had said that she was to remain in England until the following summer when she would accompany the children back to India.

The butler returned and clicked his fingers. "Come."

He led her to the hallway where the Mistress stood facing the open fire.

"I've no use for your services," the Mistress snapped, without turning around. "Your contract to accompany my grandchildren to England has been completed."

"But Curtis Sahib said …"

Red colour flooded Jamila's cheeks and her voice trailed off as the Mistress walked off, her black gown swishing on the floor. Jamila remained on the spot for a few minutes, too shocked to move.

She considered running up the grand staircase to wake the children. Perhaps Matt could talk sense into his grandmother. But then she thought better of it. She wouldn't ask the children to beg for her. She had more dignity than that.

She returned to the kitchen to collect her duffel bag. The vast space was empty except for a footman at the table drinking a cup of tea. He looked a little older than her and was so thin, his red jacket practically hung off his shoulders.

"Where will you go?" he asked.

Jamila was surprised by his interest. All the other servants had barely spoken to her. "India," she replied.

"Sounds like a good plan," he said, taking a big gulp of his tea.

She pulled out a chair and sat down. Perhaps he could help her.

"Weren't you the automobile driver who picked us up from the dock yesterday?"

He nodded.

"What's that place called?"

"Tilbury Docks," he replied. "The ships to India, Australia and America sail from there."

Dare she ask him? "Could you take me back there?"

He looked apologetic. "The Mistress wouldn't allow it. I'm sorry, the automobile only comes out on special occasions."

She wasn't surprised by his refusal. "No harm in asking, I suppose."

"I could give you directions to Tilbury, if you like," he offered. "You can take the train there."

Jamila knew she couldn't use public transport. She had no English money. "Maybe I could walk there and see a little of London on the way."

He gave her an odd look before getting up to retrieve a pencil and paper from a kitchen cabinet.

"Let me draw you a map," he said, sitting back down at the table. "We're in central London right now and you need to head east. I'll include the train route as well for when you get tired of walking."

Twenty-six miles was the distance she'd have to cover to get to the docks from Old Clover Road. Jamila thanked the footman and left the house with her duffel bag tucked under her arm. The children were still asleep.

Chapter 5

It had now been a day and a night since Jamila had left the house on Old Clover Road.

Jamila rubbed her right foot through her sock, hoping to ease the numbness. She couldn't feel her toes. Everybody she'd seen wore shoes and she was the only one wearing sandals. She ignored the pointed looks from people passing her. They didn't seem to approve of her massaging her feet in public.

She was here now. She'd walked from the house in Old Clover Road all the way to Tilbury Docks.

Jamila's resentment at her treatment had eased. She was starting to think that perhaps she'd acted too hastily and with a little too much pride. She should have woken the children and tried to find an amicable way out.

Matt was a good boy and he would have defended her. If nothing else, he'd have written to his father and ensured she was paid her wages and given a passenger ticket.

Now how was she going to get home? She didn't have a ticket or money. Perhaps the captain would allow her on board in exchange for work. She could work in the kitchens or clean the cabins. But who should she talk to?

A well-dressed man pushed her aside as he hurried towards the ship. Jamila glanced around. She was standing in the path of the landing board. It was obvious from the urgency of the passengers that the ship was going to leave soon. She joined the line.

"Where's this ship going?" she asked
the crewman checking tickets.

"It's the Atlantic line to America."

"Oh, I don't want to go there! What about India?"

"Not today."

Jamila blinked back the tears that suddenly sprang to
her eyes. "When?"

"Tuesday."

"What day is it today?"

He gave her an odd look. "Wednesday. Now get out of
the way, young lady."

Jamila's tears flowed. She couldn't help them.
She would have to wait six whole days and nights in
the cold, and she was down to her last few peanuts.
She stumbled back against the crowd and was pushed
and shoved until she was on the outside of it.

She kept moving until her back slammed up against
a wall. Feeling completely defeated, she collapsed to
the ground in a heap and buried her face in her hands.
How had her life come to this? She was penniless and
homeless in a strange country.

After a while, she sensed someone standing above her. She looked up to see a young Indian man with a head full of tight curls. A fat coil of rope was slung over his shoulder.

He must be a lascar, the name given to Indian sailors who worked on ships and docks.

"Are you all right?" he asked in a concerned voice.

She brushed her tears with the back of her hand and nodded.

He lowered the rope to the ground. "My name is Azad. May I sit?"

She shifted a little to make room for him.

"What's your name?" he asked.

She drew a long breath to steady her voice. "Jamila."

"Are you lost?"

She shook her head. "I'm exactly where I need to be."

"Where are you travelling to? India?"

She nodded.

"You're in the right place on the wrong day," Azad said.

Fresh tears gathered in her eyes. "I know."

He gave her a sympathetic look. "Don't cry. There'll be a ship to India in a few days."

Jamila brushed the tears away. "I just can't wait to get home."

"Where's that?"

"Bombay." She turned to look at him. "What about your home?"

"My house is nearby in Thurrock town."

"You live in England?" she asked, surprised.

He nodded. "I used to travel all over the world and then I met an English girl on my stopover and we got married. I gave up adventures on the seas for land."

"Do you miss it?"

"Sometimes. One day, I'll take my wife to my hometown in Goa, when we've saved up enough money. It has the most beautiful blue seas and golden sand beaches."

They were both quiet for a while, lost in their own thoughts.

The steamship's horn blew. How Jamila wished it was destined for India rather than America.

"Have you purchased your travel ticket?" Azad asked. She shook her head.

"Do you want me to point you to the ticket office? The shop sells them."

"I don't have any money," she admitted.

"Are you going to sneak on and hope you don't get discovered?" he asked.

"I was hoping that the captain might allow me to work on the ship," she said, with as much enthusiasm as she could muster. "I'm very good at cleaning, cooking and looking after children."

Azad looked doubtful. "I don't think it works like that. You'd have to apply for the job with the shipping company." Azad cocked his head to the side. "I think I know what your story is."

"How would you know?"

"Because you aren't the first Indian girl to sit stranded on this dock, thousands of miles away from home," he said. "You're an abandoned ayah, aren't you?"

She looked at him in surprise. "There are others like me from India? Ayahs?"

He nodded.

"Where are they? What happened to them?"

Azad ran his fingers through his curly hair. "Well … that's a long story, but why don't you come with me."

Jamila hesitated. Her instinct was telling her to be careful. She'd heard stories in Bombay of young girls being kidnapped by strangers. What if this man was going to take her somewhere and lock her up? What if he'd just made that stuff up about an English wife in Thurrock town. How could she trust him? She'd only met him 15 minutes ago. Perhaps she should just wait here at the dock. She'd survived one night already on the streets. What was another few?

"Are you coming?" Azad asked.

Jamila bit her lip. What should she do?

Chapter 6

Jamila decided it was safer to remain at the port than to leave for an unknown location. Her Ammi had always warned her about keeping safe and one lesson was not to go off with strangers, no matter how kind they appeared.

Thankfully, Azad accepted her refusal with a shrug and walked off. He returned a few minutes later with a chunk of bread. She took it gratefully and chewed.

"I'll see you later today," Azad said. "Don't move. I want to introduce you to someone who can help."

She nodded, her mouth full.

The hours passed and Jamila watched the steamship prepare for its departure. The steam chugged out of its funnel and the horn hooted. When it finally glided away for America, a smaller ship took its place. Lascars working on the port ran forward to unload the heavy crates and boxes.

She wondered where this small ship had sailed from. The British Empire covered one fifth of the earth and she knew goods arrived in England from all these countries.

It was late afternoon when Azad returned, this time with a middle-aged Indian lady in tow who was dressed in a white sari and blue cardigan. Hope rose in Jamila's chest. Perhaps this lady could help her board a ship.

"Jamila, this is Asha," Azad introduced. "She is from the Ayahs' Home. It's a place where abandoned ayahs are given shelter."

"Nice to meet you, Jamila," Asha said warmly.

"I don't want to go back into London city," Jamila blurted. "I want to board the ship to India."

"We'll help you get home," Asha said. "The summer holidays are coming to an end and families will be travelling back to their jobs in India. They come to the Home to employ ayahs. You'll be snapped up."

Jamila was still reluctant to leave the port. "Can't I wait here to be chosen?"

"Under the stars, all alone?" Asha asked. "You've been very lucky that no harm has come to you so far. Come with me and I promise you that we'll find a family for you this Tuesday."

Jamila tucked a stray strand of hair behind her ear. Should she trust this lady? Was there really such a thing as an Ayahs' Home?

Asha sensed Jamila's reluctance. Reaching into her shoulder bag, she pulled out a newspaper cutting and handed it to Jamila. "The London paper wrote about the Ayahs' Home in an article about charities. Please have a look. You will see me there, centre stage."

Jamila picked up her duffel bag, her mind made up. "I'll go with you."

Asha nodded happily before turning to Azad. "You've saved another girl from destitution and misery."

Jamila opened her mouth to add her thanks but the lump in her throat prevented it. She could tell from the look in Azad's eyes that he understood and didn't need the words.

It was evening by the time Asha stopped outside 4 King Edward Road. It had taken them an hour and a half on two buses to complete the journey from the dock.

Jamila gazed at the house.

Asha pushed open the solid black door and marched briskly to a large front room where five Indian women, dressed in white saris and cardigans, were reading or doing needlework.

"This is Jamila," Asha announced.

The women, who all looked a lot older than Jamila, waved or called out a greeting.

"How many ayahs live here?" Jamila asked in a small voice.

"About 100 a year," Asha replied. "Of course, not all have been abandoned. Some are experienced travellers who lodge here while they wait for a new family. Mrs Saxena has travelled 30 times back and forth."

Mrs Saxena shook her head. She had the air of a very strict ayah. "The next trip will be my thirtieth."

Jamila perched down on the sofa.

"Would you like a bath and a hot meal?" Asha asked.

"That would be really nice, thank you," Jamila replied, unable to keep the slight tremble out of her voice. She felt overwhelmed by the kindness. Ammi always said there were good people in the world. Sometimes, you just had to look for them.

Chapter 7

"How will we find her in this crowd?" Lizzie demanded.

The three children glanced around at Tilbury Docks. There were people everywhere. Passengers rushing to board the steamship, servants handing over luggage to the lascars, and tradespeople trying to sell their goods.

On the day that Jamila had been dismissed, the children had quizzed all the servants. They claimed not to know where she intended to go. The children guessed they had been sworn to secrecy by Granny. It had taken a couple of days, but they finally managed to crack the footman with an offer of chocolate. Munching on the bar, he'd told them that their ayah was headed towards Tilbury Docks. On that Thursday, they informed Granny they were going to play at the park, and instead made their way to the East End by London underground and then the bus. It had taken just over an hour.

"Lizzie, don't let go of my hand," Matt instructed. "Do you understand?"

She tightened her grip and nodded.

"Let's split up," Alex said. "I'll search for Jamila on board and you two keep a watch from here."

"You don't have a ticket," Matt reminded him. "How are you going to get on board?"

"Watch me," Alex grinned and ran off.

"Where do you think you're going?"

A voice stopped Alex in his tracks. He turned to face the ticket inspector with his haughtiest look. It was one of Granny's favourite expressions and she always got her way when she wore it. "On board," he said, in a voice to match the look.

"Ticket, please."

"Do I look like I carry the paperwork?" Alex retorted. "Papa has them and he's already on board. I arrived here in the second horse-carriage. Obviously, Papa didn't wait for me. He's probably having words with the captain now. They're old school friends."

The inspector's eyes darted nervously to the left and right. "But Master – "

"Alexander Frederick Curtis," he provided. "Look, Papa has the power to have the ship turned back to dock if he finds out I'm not on board. And what's your name? I'll be sure to report the crewman who prevented me from boarding. I'm sure your captain won't be impressed."

"Oh, go on then," the inspector said, with a jerk of his head. "I didn't see you."

Alex sauntered up the landing board. Once on deck, he broke into a run, dodging the passengers who were milling about. Some stood at the railing, waving down at people on the dock. Some went in search of their cabins. Some shouted at the lascars to hurry with their luggage. It was as chaotic on deck as it was down on the dock.

"Jamila!" Alex called out. "Jamila!"

"Stop shouting, boy," an old, stooped woman ordered, waving her walking stick at him.

"I'm looking for my ayah."

"I saw an Indian girl earlier," she said, pointing her stick to the left. "In the direction of crew quarters."

"Thank you." Alex sped down towards the cabins. What was Jamila doing there?

50

"Jamila!" he shouted, popping his head around the first door in the lower corridor. It was a tiny room with a table, round window and a door on the opposite end. Alex crossed the space in three strides and yanked it open, curious to see where it would lead. Apparently nowhere, he thought, as he stared at the shelves packed with towels and bedsheets. This was a storeroom. He turned back to the main door and pulled. It didn't budge.

"Agh!" he yelled in frustration, trying again. It was locked. Just his luck to get trapped inside a giant cupboard. Now what? He began to bang on the door. "Help! Help!" Seconds passed which became long minutes. "Help!"

Nobody came to his rescue. Why would they? He was in a cupboard in a lone corridor while every crew member was on deck helping the passengers.

The bellow of the ship's horn made him jump. If he wasn't rescued in the next few minutes, he'd be on his way to India. Alex began to hammer on the door and then stopped as a thought occurred to him. Would it be so bad to return to India? He loved it there. It was an exciting and adventurous place, which was why so many English people lived there. Why shouldn't he return there to be with his parents? All he had to do was hide out for the next three to four weeks on this ship. Then he thought of Matt and Lizzie. They'd be lonely without him, and they also needed to find Jamila. He didn't want his ayah to think he'd played a part in the way she was treated. Mother always said people should be treated with respect, from the Emperor King to the servants.

He had to do something. Alex twisted the window handle. The relief he felt when it opened wide disappeared when he peered out. The deck below looked a long way down and he'd break a leg if he attempted to jump.

What now? Then he remembered the bedsheets.
He yanked open the cupboard and pulled
the top bedsheet. A whole stack of sheets came tumbling
down and around him. Mentally saying sorry to
the maid who would have to clean up, he grabbed three
sheets and began to tie them together.

He then took one end and dropped to his knees
to secure it to the table leg closest to the window.
Thankfully, the table was nailed to the floor which
meant it wouldn't move. Picking up the other end, he
threw the sheet out of the window. It didn't quite reach
the deck floor, but it wasn't too far off the ground.
Alex was confident that he'd be able to jump the last bit
without harm to himself.

Taking a deep breath, he clutched his makeshift rope and crawled out of the window.

He'd climbed plenty of trees near Granny's country house and even scaled a palm tree on Bombay beach. He could do this. Slowly and carefully, he began his descent.

Back at the dock, Matt and Lizzie, unaware that their brother was hanging in mid-air on a rope of bedsheets, continued their own search for Jamila. There were fewer crowds now as most of the passengers were on board the ship. Only those last to arrive were scrambling in a hurry.

"Look!" Lizzie shouted in excitement. "Is that her?"

Matt's eyes swivelled in the direction of Lizzie's pointed finger. He saw the back of a woman dressed in a sari. It wasn't white in colour, but she was slim and the same height as Jamila. Perhaps it was her.

They raced forward until they were standing in front of her, blocking her path.

Disappointment came crashing down.

It wasn't Jamila.

The woman, well dressed and clearly not a servant, raised a brow in inquiry.

"Sorry," Matt apologised, moving to the side.
He turned to Lizzie with a worried frown. "Isn't it strange that there aren't many Indian passengers on this ship?"

Lizzie looked up at him. "Do you think this ship is going somewhere else and not India?"

Alarm filled Matt's eyes and he broke into a run towards the gangway. "Alex needs to get off that ship!"

Back on the ship, Alex had managed to attract a crowd below him.

"Oi, you!" a voice yelled.

Alex peered down. Men dressed in white trousers and belted red tunics were looking up at him. That must be the deck where the engine rooms were located, and the men must be the lascars who operated the engine, he thought.

"Just coming," Alex called, as if this was the most normal situation in the world.

"What do you think you're doing?" the tallest lascar demanded.

Alex jumped the last few feet. "I got locked up there and had no other way down," he explained. "Otherwise, I'd be on my way to India with you all."

The lascars laughed. "We aren't going to India," the tall one said. "This ship is headed to Australia, so unless you want to come with us down under, I suggest you get off this ship right now."

"Where should I run?" Alex cried, panicking.

"To the stairs at the end of this corridor," the tall lascar advised. "Up two storeys to the main deck. Run to the right and you'll come across a landing board. Hurry!"

He sped up to the main deck and pushed against the crowds of passengers surging in the opposite direction.

Finally, he reached the landing board. "I'm not a passenger, let me off!"

The crewman scowled at him before stepping aside. Alex ran as fast as he could to an anxious-looking Matt and Lizzie.

"What happened?" Matt demanded.

"Got locked in a cupboard," Alex gasped, trying to catch his breath. "I had to use bedsheets to climb down."

Matt stared in shock and then shrugged. Nothing ever surprised him about his reckless twin.

"I asked a crewman where this ship was heading," Matt said. "You're never going to believe it."

"I know," Alex said.

"You do?" Lizzie piped up.

"Australia," Alex said, shaking his head. It was a good thing he escaped when he did. Imagine that. Any longer in that storeroom and he'd be on his way to the other side of the world.

"I don't know why we thought all ships from here only sail to India," Matt said. "Anyway, the next ship to Bombay will dock here on Tuesday. We'll come back then."

"Where do you think Jamila is now?" Lizzie asked, her expression full of worry. She'd been so sure they'd find Jamila here today.

"I don't know," Matt admitted. "But I hope she's found a place to be safe."

Chapter 8

"I think we've got plenty of time to look for Jamila," Matt said looking around at the near-empty dock.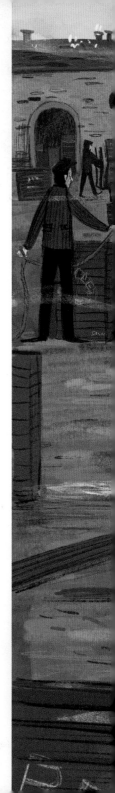

It was Tuesday and the ship was scheduled to sail to India just after noon. They had plenty of time to spot Jamila. They'd left the house after breakfast and were hoping to find her today as school started tomorrow. Thankfully, Granny had left them with the servants for a few days. She'd had important matters to resolve at her country house in Derbyshire.

"You will behave when I'm gone, won't you," she'd said in a tone that was clear that she was making a statement rather than asking them.

They'd nodded, hardly able to keep the glee off their faces. A few whole days without Granny's strict rules and regulations was the best thing that could happen. It freed them up to search for Jamila at the dock without having to come up with an elaborate story about where they were going to disappear to for the day.

They took up position near the ship's landing board, eyes peeled for their ayah. The minutes turned into hours and passengers slowly arrived to board the ship.

"Good afternoon."

They looked up at an Indian man with a head full of tight curls.

"Are you looking for someone?" the man asked. "I've noticed you've been standing here since this morning."

"Yes, we are," Matt replied. "But who are you?"

"I'm Azad," he said. "What are your names?"

"I'm Lizzie and these are my brothers Matt and Alex," Lizzie said.

A flash of recognition crossed Azad's face, but it vanished just as quickly. "Very nice to meet you," he said, bowing his head to Lizzie.

"You might be able to help us," Matt said. "Have you seen an Indian girl? She dresses in a white sari and is about 19 years old."

"What's her name?"

"Jamila, she's our ayah."

"And Granny dismissed her," Lizzie added.

"Why did your granny do that?" Azad wanted to know.

"Because we aren't babies anymore and we don't need her," Lizzie blurted.

Alex poked Lizzie's arm.

"Ow!" she yelped.

"Why are you looking for her if you don't need her?" Azad asked.

"Because we want her to come back," Lizzie said rubbing her arm.

Azad turned to Alex and Matt. "Tell me, has she visited England before?"

"No," Matt replied. "It was her first time."

"So, she was in a new, strange country for less than 24 hours," Azad said slowly. "And then she was thrown out of your house?"

Alex had had enough of what sounded very much like an interrogation. "Look, mister," he said, hands on his hips. "*We* didn't throw her out. Our granny did, and we began the search for her as soon as we found out. We know what happened to her was wrong and we're here to make everything right!"

Azad smiled. It seemed Alex's words were just what he needed to hear. "I did meet Jamila, and she told me about her three charges. I guessed who you three were when – " His voice trailed away as he watched Lizzie bolt into the crowd.

Chapter 9

"Lizzie! Stop!" Matt yelled, chasing after her. Alex and Azad followed.

Lizzie ignored Matt and pushed past people before flinging herself at a slim figure in a white sari. "I knew it was you!"

It was Jamila! They'd found her at last.

Matt and Alex whooped with joy as they wrapped their arms around her waist.

Jamila hugged them back before disentangling herself from their grip. "What are you doing here?"

"We've been looking for you!" Lizzie cried.

"Why?"

Her question stumped them. "Because we missed you," Matt offered at last. "Granny had no right to dismiss you and we're so sorry for the way you were treated."

"It's not your fault," Jamila said, shrugging. "You don't have to apologise."

"Please come home with us," Alex pleaded.

There was a catch in Jamila's voice. "I can't."

Lizzie's lower lip trembled. "Why?"

"What choice do I have?" Jamila asked, her voice a little higher than usual. "Your granny refuses to keep me on, and a new Sahib has already employed me. His driver has just brought me here and his children are waiting for me on the ship." Her eyes suddenly flashed with a memory. "I insisted on receiving my wages in advance of the journey this time."

"Jamila," Matt whispered, reaching for her hand.

She snatched it away. "Your granny had no right," she blurted, unable to contain the hurt at her treatment any longer. "She made me penniless and homeless. I could have been killed in the streets of London and my body thrown into the River Thames."

They stared at her, at a loss for words.

"And do you know the worst part?" Jamila demanded. "I was worried you wouldn't miss me because you're all grown up and don't need me anymore!"

"Of course we missed you," they chorused, without hesitation.

It made her feel better and she gave them a small smile, her outrage forgotten.

Lizzie suddenly remembered something and tugged at Matt's arm. "Give it to her."

Matt reached into his trouser pocket to pull out an envelope. "Father asked us to pass this to Granny. It's your wages. Granny was supposed to give you the money but – " His voice trailed off.

There was no need to repeat Granny's actions. It was more important to put matters right. That's why the twins had sneaked into the study and taken the unopened envelope of money.

Jamila bit her lip. She felt a pang of shame for doubting their father's trustworthiness. She'd always known Sahib Curtis to be a good person and a good employer.

"Thank you." Her hand closed around the envelope, and she bent down to hug each of them. "Now I must go."

"No!" Lizzie's tears spilt over.

Jamila bent down again for a second hug. "Lizzie, please try to understand. I must accompany these other children back to India. I'm their ayah now."

"You're right," Matt said. "You need to do what's right for you, and not what we want you to do. We were searching for you because we thought you needed to be rescued. But you don't need us. We're happy that you're happy."

Alex nodded. "As long as you're happy, Jamila. Maybe you'll let us visit you when we return to India."

Jamila nodded. "I'd love to see you again. We'll play cricket on Bombay beach just like before."

Lizzie wiped her tears with the back of her hand.

"Where's your handkerchief?" Jamila said. "Memsahib would scold me if she saw you do that."

"Mother's not here to see," Matt said, doing a scary impression of their grandmother. "She sent us to live with her dragon mother."

"Matt!" Jamila protested. "You shouldn't talk about your granny like that."

"Well, it's true," he muttered.

Jamila looked over their heads at Azad who'd been standing silently. "You were sent as my protector. I wouldn't have survived on my own. Thank you."

Azad smiled. "Safe journey, Jamila. And if you ever come back to these shores, be sure to find me on this dock."

"I will return," Jamila promised. "I have friends at the Ayahs' Home, and I intend to follow the footsteps of my new friend Mrs Saxena. She told me I don't have to remain attached to one Sahib's family. This way maybe I'll be able to have the adventures I always wanted. Maybe I'll get to visit the Scottish Highlands, the Welsh valleys and see the English countryside too."

"Will you come and see us too?" Lizzie asked.

"Of course I will," Jamila replied. "When your granny isn't home though."

They all laughed, and then Jamila pressed her hand on her heart in the Muslim practice of greeting and goodbye. Azad returned the gesture and the children copied.

Managing a final, wonky smile through shining tears, Jamila turned to walk away.

Once she reached the deck, she bent down to greet four small children. Then she disappeared within the crowd of passengers.

"She's their ayah now," Lizzie said bravely.

"Yes, they need her more than we do," Matt agreed, squeezing his sister's hand. "But she'll always be our friend."

They waited on the bank until the ship was ready to leave. Slowly, she slipped away from the port, and they scanned the deck for a last glimpse of Jamila in case she was one of the hundreds of passengers lining the railing.

"There!" Alex shouted. "Look, there she is. She's come back."

And she had. Jamila's arms waved from side to side in goodbye, and they waved back until she was a speck in the distance.

"We should plan our trip to India," Alex said.
"And the list should include visiting Jamila."

Jamila's diary

Dear Diary

　It's my second day at the Ayahs' Home, and some of the anxiety has eased. The other ayahs are so friendly and they've taken me under their wing. My favourite has to be Mrs Saxena. She's so worldly and independent.

　I can't stop thinking about what she said about her next trip to India. It'll be her thirtieth voyage across the sea. Perhaps I too could travel back and forth from India with children who need to be accompanied. Maybe I could have a career just like hers.

This thought makes me feel better and more hopeful for the future. It makes me believe that my journey to England wasn't a bad idea, or that I should give up on all my dreams because of one horrible experience.

I've decided that I'm going to put my feelings of resentment towards the children's granny aside. If I've learned a lesson, it's that some people will treat me badly, but I must never let them defeat me. I must pull myself together and carry on.

I'm sad that I never got to say goodbye to Matt, Alex and Lizzie. Who knows, maybe I will see them again when they visit their parents in India? That is if I'm at home and not off travelling around Great Britain's Empire myself.

If Mrs Saxena can do it, then so can I.

I'm determined to dream again.

Ideas for reading

Written by Gill Matthews
Primary Literacy Consultant

Reading objectives:
- check that the book makes sense to them, discussing their understanding and exploring the meaning of words in context
- ask questions to improve their understanding
- draw inferences such as inferring characters' feelings, thoughts and motives from their actions, and justify inferences with evidence

Spoken language objectives:
- articulate and justify answers, arguments and opinions
- give well-structured descriptions, explanations and narratives for different purposes, including for expressing feelings
- participate in discussions, presentations, performances, role play, improvisations and debates

Curriculum links: History – a study of an aspect or theme in British history that extends pupils' chronological knowledge beyond 1066; Relationships education – the importance of respecting others, even when they are very different from them (for example, physically, in character, personality or backgrounds), or make different choices or have different preferences or beliefs

Interest words: glancing, steadied, subsided, tentatively, shifted

Resources: IT

Build a context for reading

- Look at the front cover. Ask children what details they can see and who they think Jamila might be.
- Read the blurb together and discuss what they think an ayah might be.
- Ask children why they think Matt, Alex and Lizzie's parents didn't bring them home from India themselves. Discuss the phrase *the children know they must find her* and what this shows about the children.
- Draw attention to the type of story this is and establish that people, places and attitudes change over time.